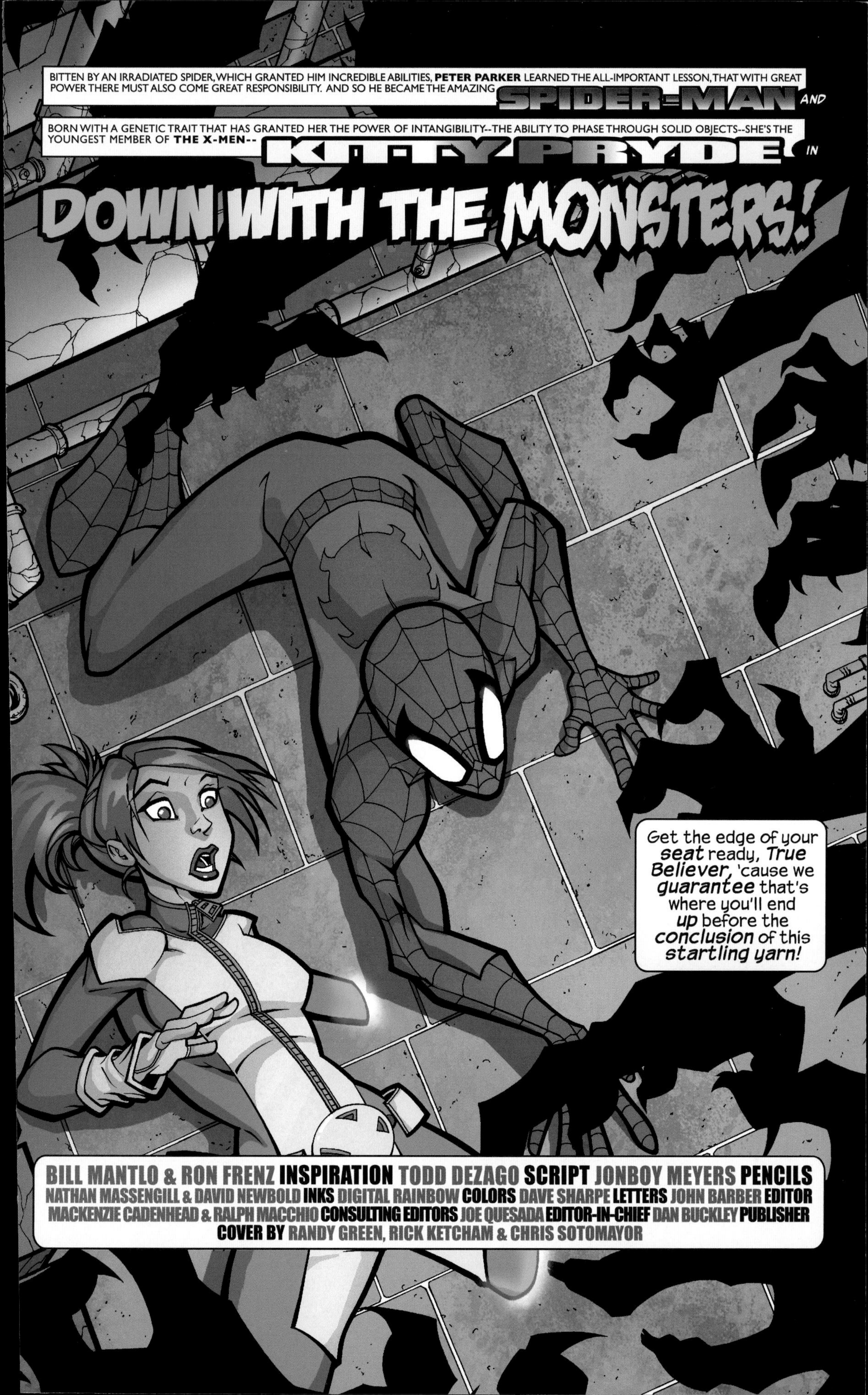

BITTEN BY AN IRRADIATED SPIDER, WHICH GRANTED HIM INCREDIBLE ABILITIES, PETER PARKER LEARNED THE ALL-IMPORTANT LESSON, THAT WITH GREAT POWER THERE MUST ALSO COME GREAT RESPONSIBILITY. AND SO HE BECAME THE AMAZING
SPIDER-MAN AND
BORN WITH A GENETIC TRAIT THAT HAS GRANTED HER THE POWER OF INTANGIBILITY--THE ABILITY TO PHASE THROUGH SOLID OBJECTS--SHE'S THE YOUNGEST MEMBER OF THE X-MEN--
KITTY PRYDE IN
DOWN WITH THE MONSTERS!
Get the edge of your seat ready, True Believer, 'cause we guarantee that's where you'll end up before the conclusion of this startling yarn!
BILL MANTLO & RON FRENZ INSPIRATION TODD DEZAGO SCRIPT JONBOY MEYERS PENCILS
NATHAN MASSENGILL & DAVID NEWBOLD INKS DIGITAL RAINBOW COLORS DAVE SHARPE LETTERS JOHN BARBER EDITOR
MACKENZIE CADENHEAD & RALPH MACCHIO CONSULTING EDITORS JOE QUESADA EDITOR-IN-CHIEF DAN BUCKLEY PUBLISHER
COVER BY RANDY GREEN, RICK KETCHAM & CHRIS SOTOMAYOR

VISIT US AT
www.abdopub.com

Spotlight, a division of ABDO Publishing Company Inc., is the school and library distributor of the Marvel Entertainment books.

Library bound edition © 2006

Library of Congress Cataloging-in-Publication Data

Spider-Man and Kitty Pryde in Down With the Monsters!

ISBN 1-59961-002-7   (Reinforced Library Bound Edition)

All Spotlight books are reinforced library binding and manufactured in the United States of America

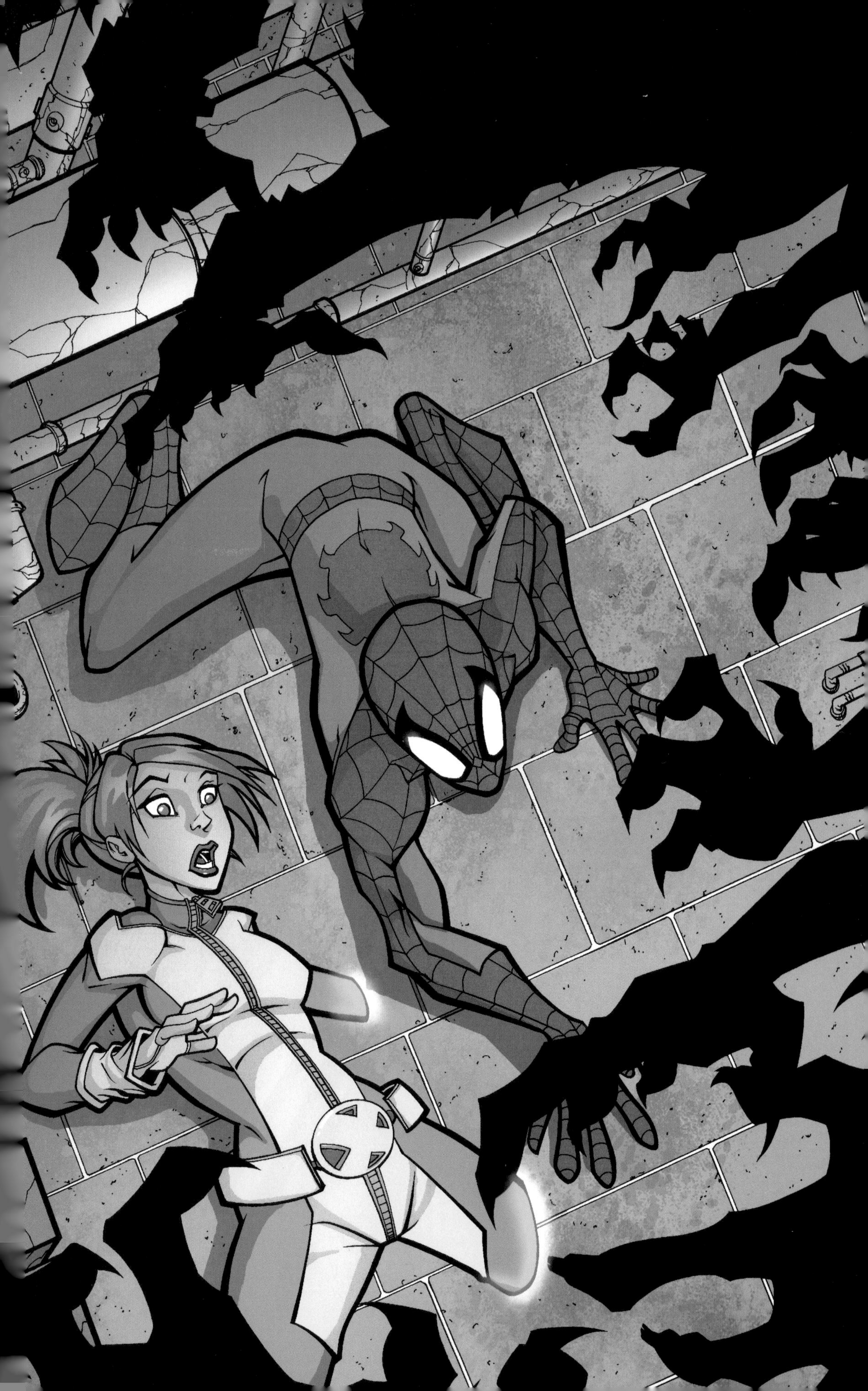

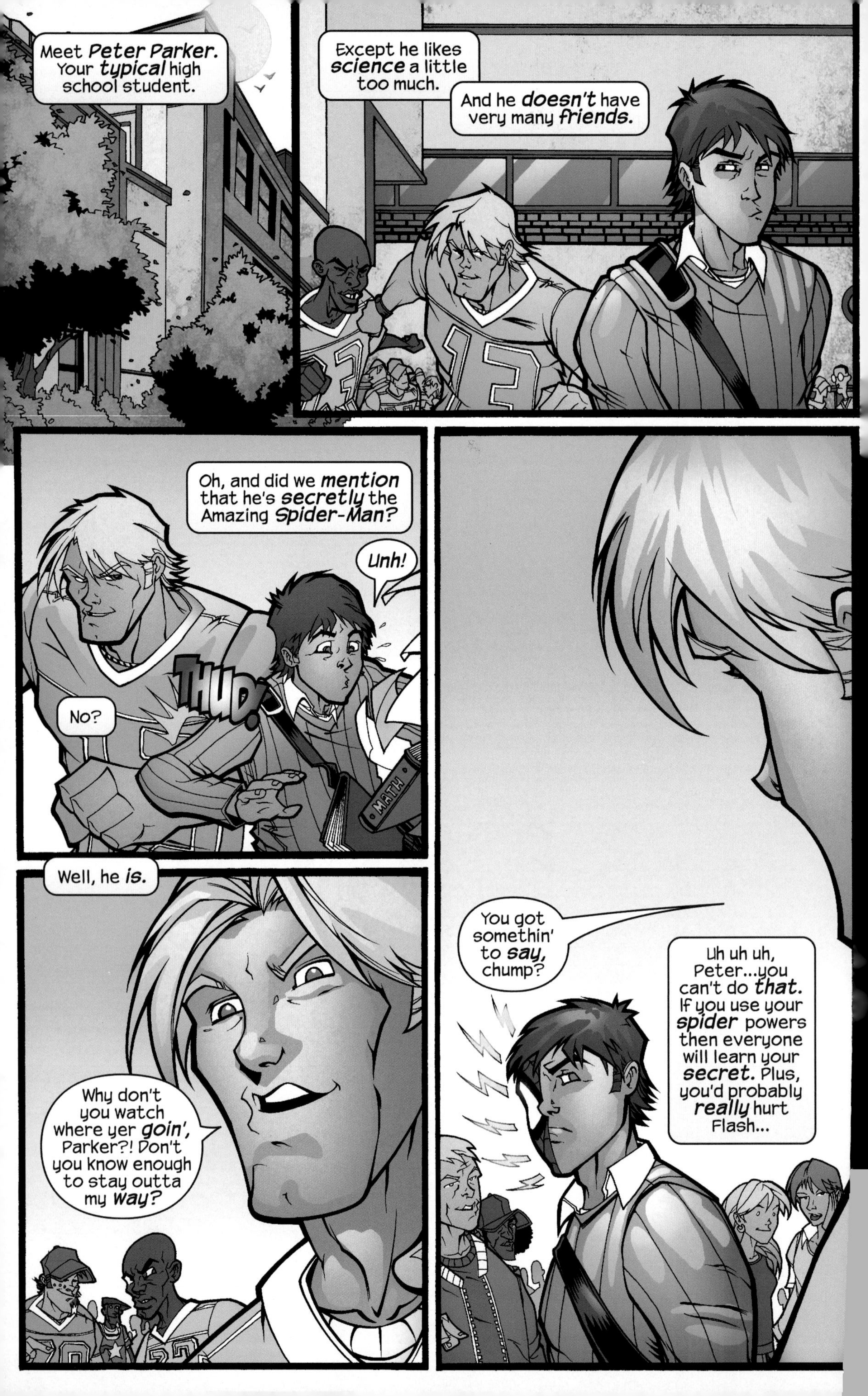

Meet Peter Parker. Your typical high school student.
Except he likes science a little too much.
And he doesn't have very many friends.
Oh, and did we mention that he's secretly the Amazing Spider-Man?
Unh!
THUD!
No?
MATH
Well, he is.
Why don't you watch where yer goin', Parker?! Don't you know enough to stay outta my way?
You got somethin' to say, chump?
Uh uh uh, Peter...you can't do that. If you use your spider powers then everyone will learn your secret. Plus, you'd probably really hurt Flash...

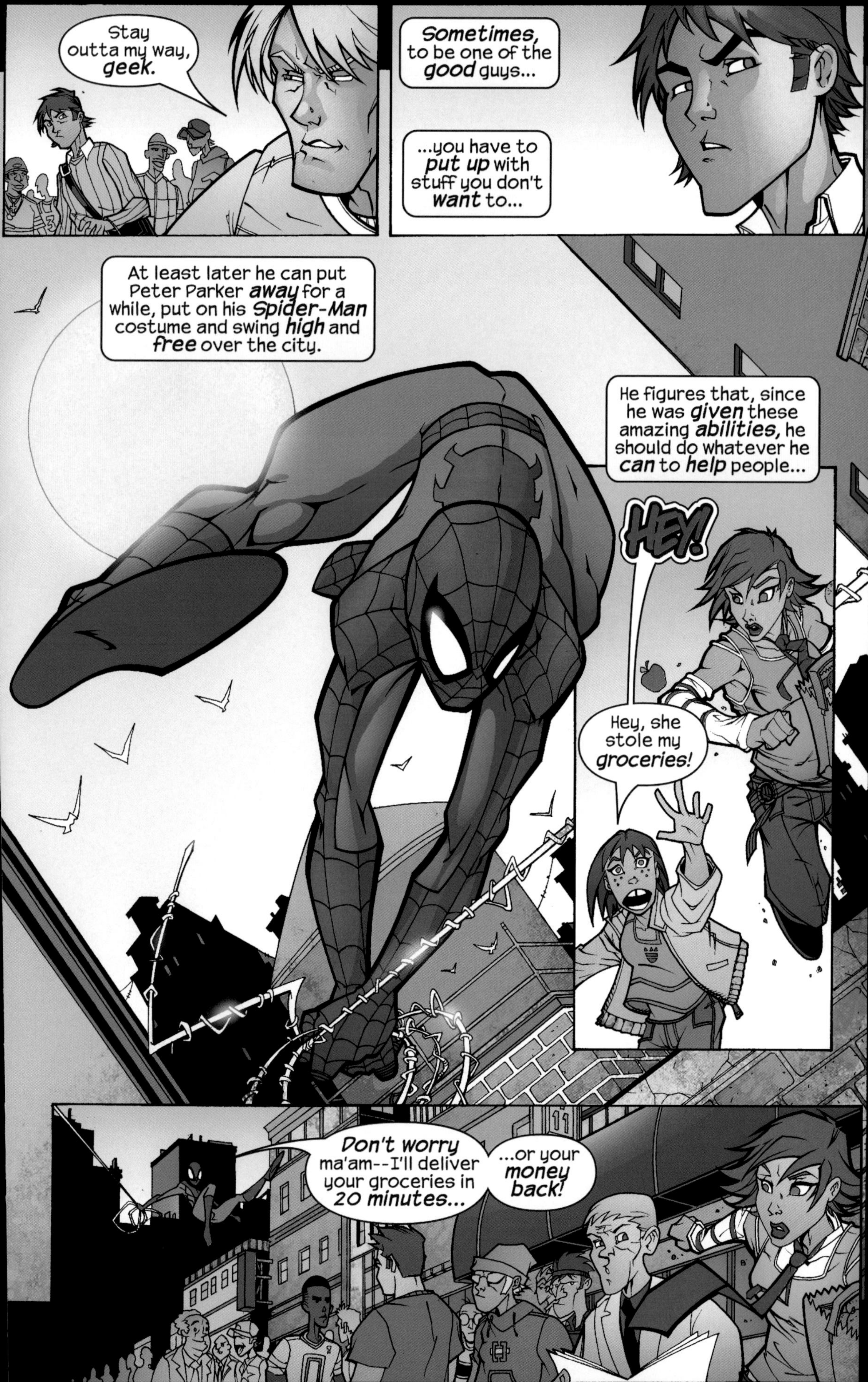
Stay outta my way, geek.
Sometimes, to be one of the good guys...
...you have to put up with stuff you don't want to...
At least later he can put Peter Parker away for a while, put on his Spider-Man costume and swing high and free over the city.
He figures that, since he was given these amazing abilities, he should do whatever he can to help people...
HEY!
Hey, she stole my groceries!
Don't worry ma'am--I'll deliver your groceries in 20 minutes...
...or your money back!

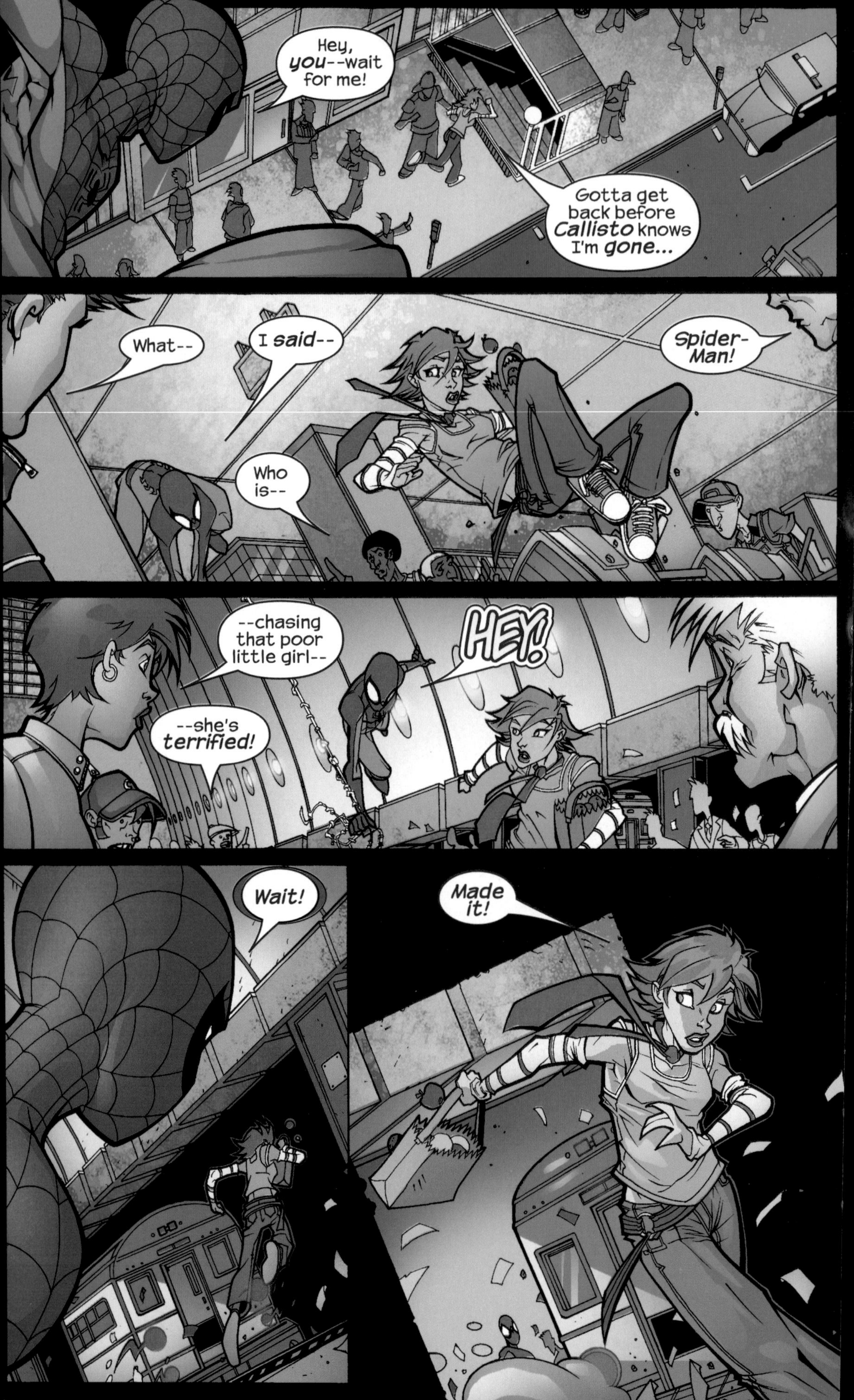
Hey, you--wait for me!
Gotta get back before Callisto knows I'm gone...
What--
I said--
Spider-Man!
Who is--
--chasing that poor little girl--
HEY!
--she's terrified!
Wait!
Made it!

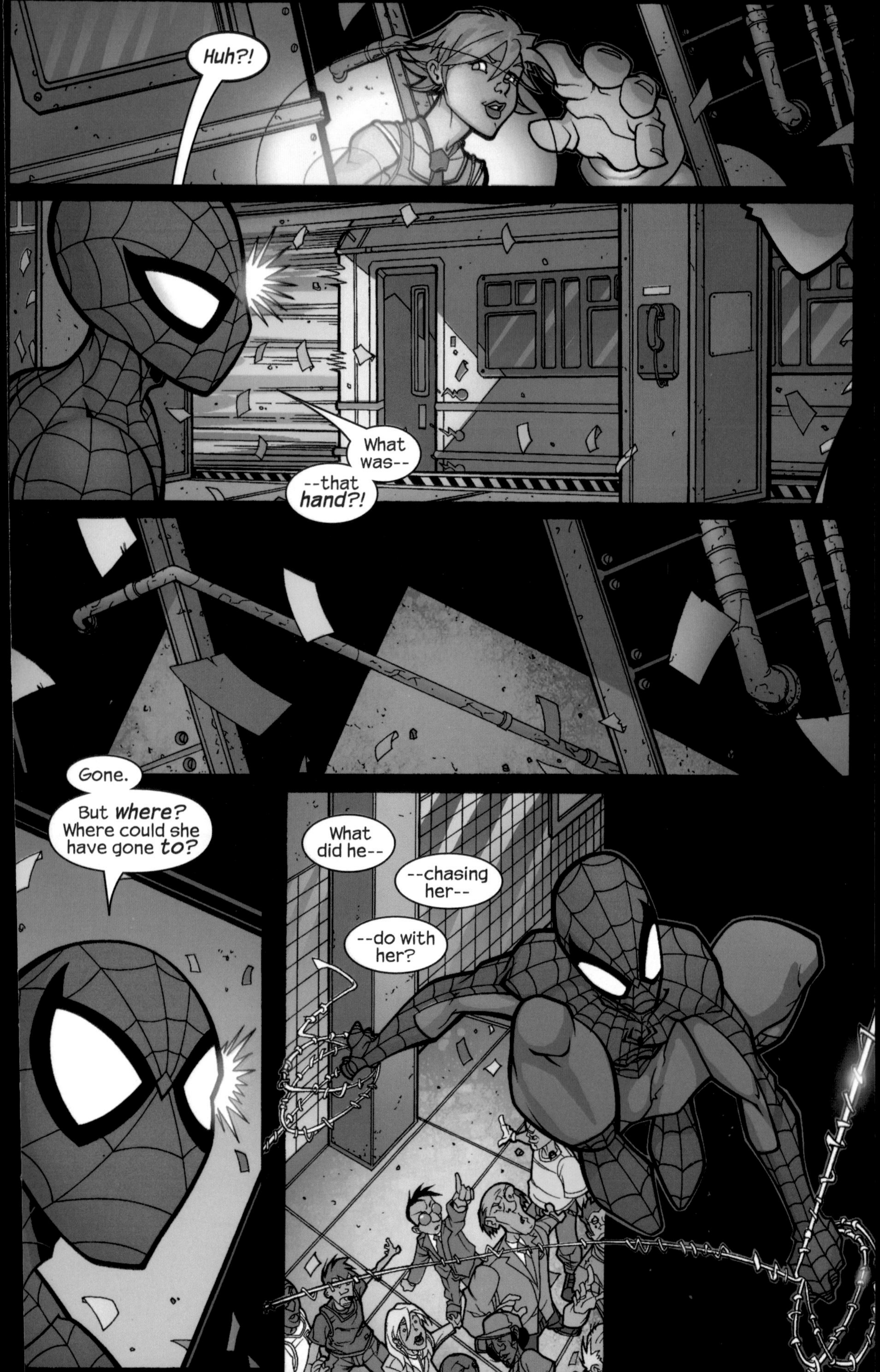
Huh?!
What was--
--that hand?!
Gone.
But where? Where could she have gone to?
What did he--
--chasing her--
--do with her?

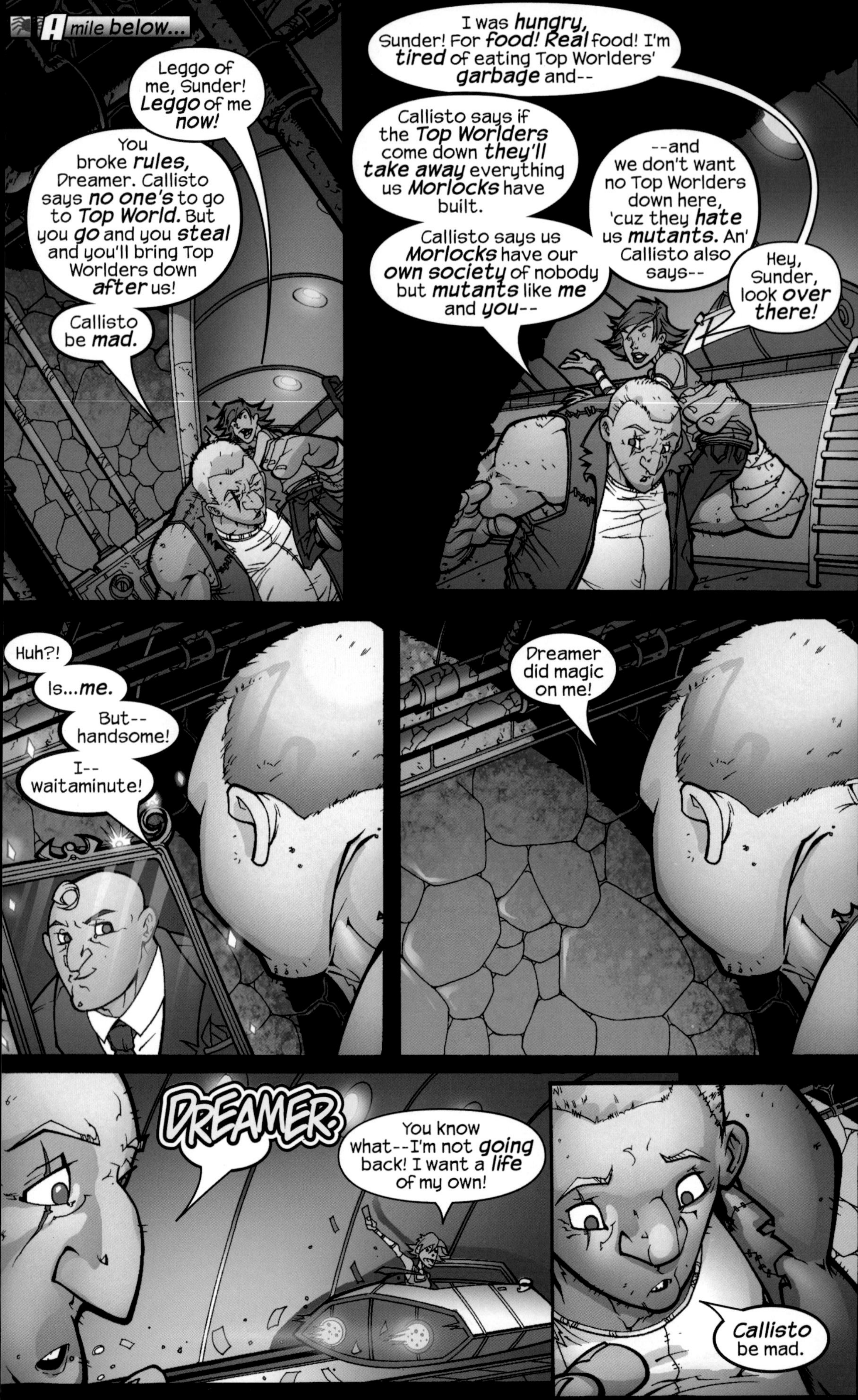
A mile below...
Leggo of me, Sunder! Leggo of me now!
You broke rules, Dreamer. Callisto says no one's to go to Top World. But you go and you steal and you'll bring Top Worlders down after us!
Callisto be mad.
I was hungry, Sunder! For food! Real food! I'm tired of eating Top Worlders' garbage and--
Callisto says if the Top Worlders come down they'll take away everything us Morlocks have built.
Callisto says us Morlocks have our own society of nobody but mutants like me and you--
--and we don't want no Top Worlders down here, 'cuz they hate us mutants. An' Callisto also says--
Hey, Sunder, look over there!
Huh?!
Is...me.
But-- handsome!
I-- waitaminute!
Dreamer did magic on me!
DREAMER.
You know what--I'm not going back! I want a life of my own!
Callisto be mad.

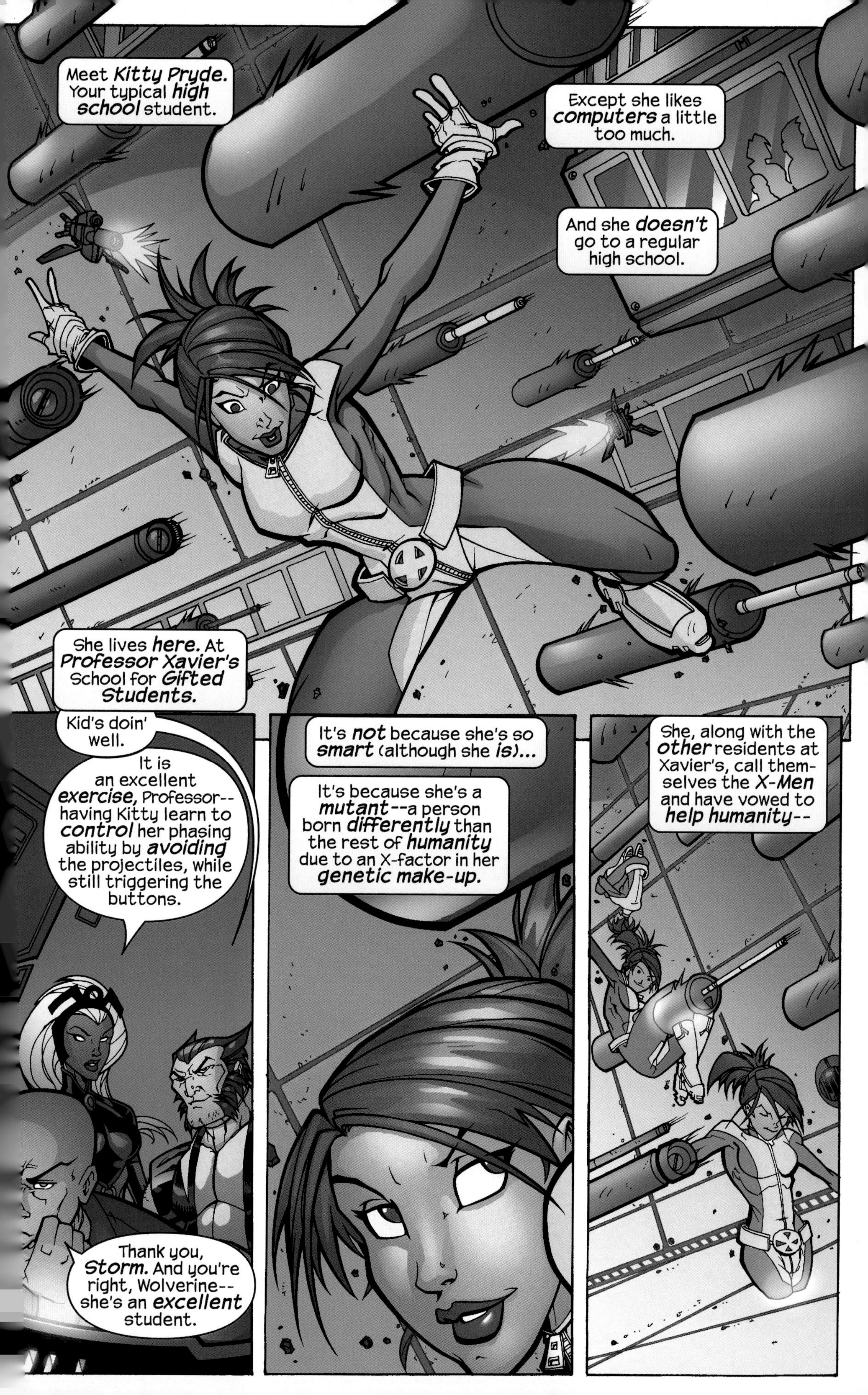
Meet Kitty Pryde. Your typical high school student.
Except she likes computers a little too much.
And she doesn't go to a regular high school.
She lives here. At Professor Xavier's School for Gifted Students.
Kid's doin' well.
It is an excellent exercise, Professor--having Kitty learn to control her phasing ability by avoiding the projectiles, while still triggering the buttons.
Thank you, Storm. And you're right, Wolverine--she's an excellent student.
It's not because she's so smart (although she is)...
It's because she's a mutant--a person born differently than the rest of humanity due to an X-factor in her genetic make-up.
She, along with the other residents at Xavier's, call themselves the X-Men and have vowed to help humanity--

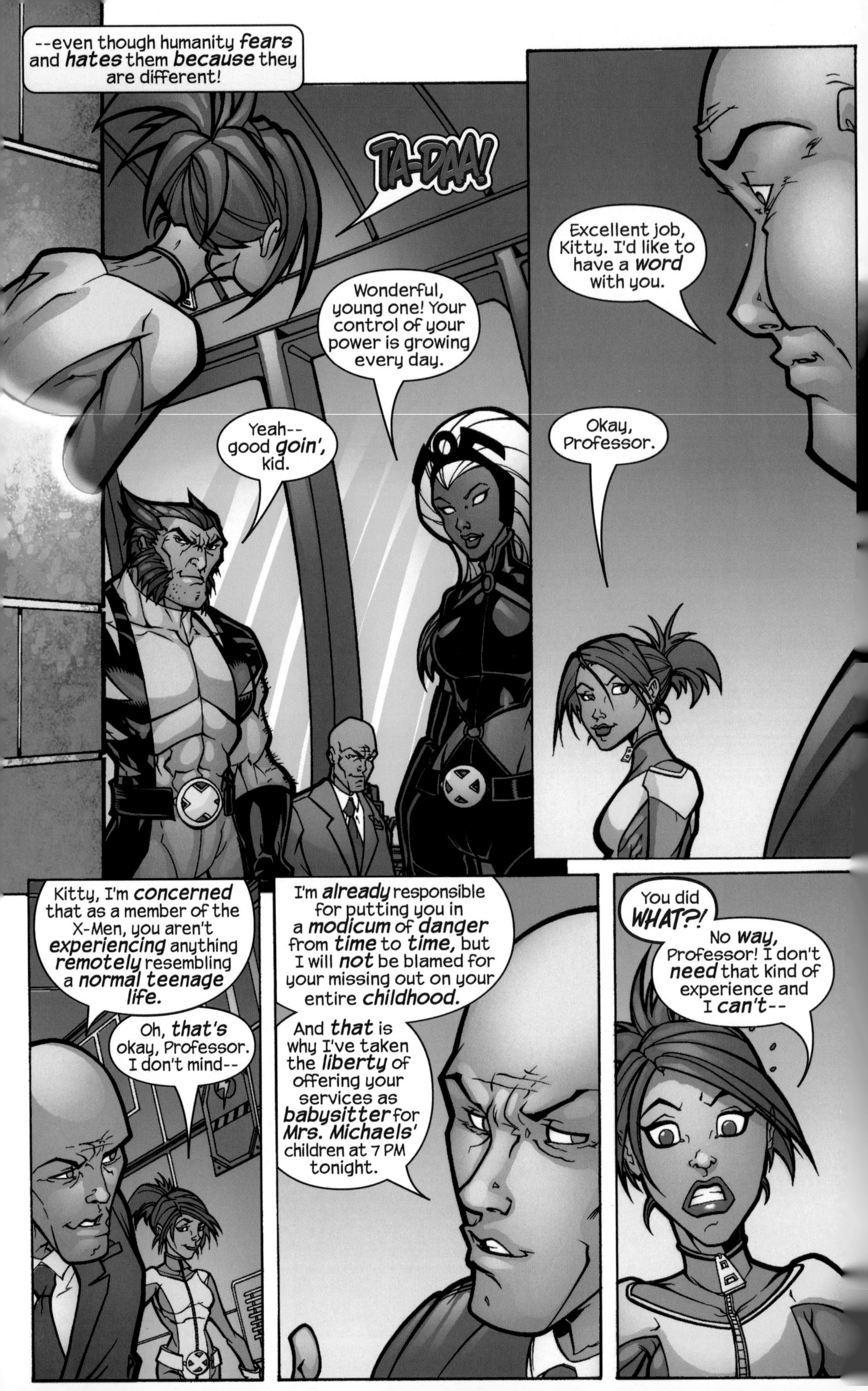
--even though humanity fears and hates them because they are different!
TA-DAA!
Wonderful, young one! Your control of your power is growing every day.
Yeah--good goin', kid.
Excellent job, Kitty. I'd like to have a word with you.
Okay, Professor.
Kitty, I'm concerned that as a member of the X-Men, you aren't experiencing anything remotely resembling a normal teenage life.
Oh, that's okay, Professor. I don't mind--
I'm already responsible for putting you in a modicum of danger from time to time, but I will not be blamed for your missing out on your entire childhood.
And that is why I've taken the liberty of offering your services as babysitter for Mrs. Michaels' children at 7 PM tonight.
You did WHAT?!
No way, Professor! I don't need that kind of experience and I can't--

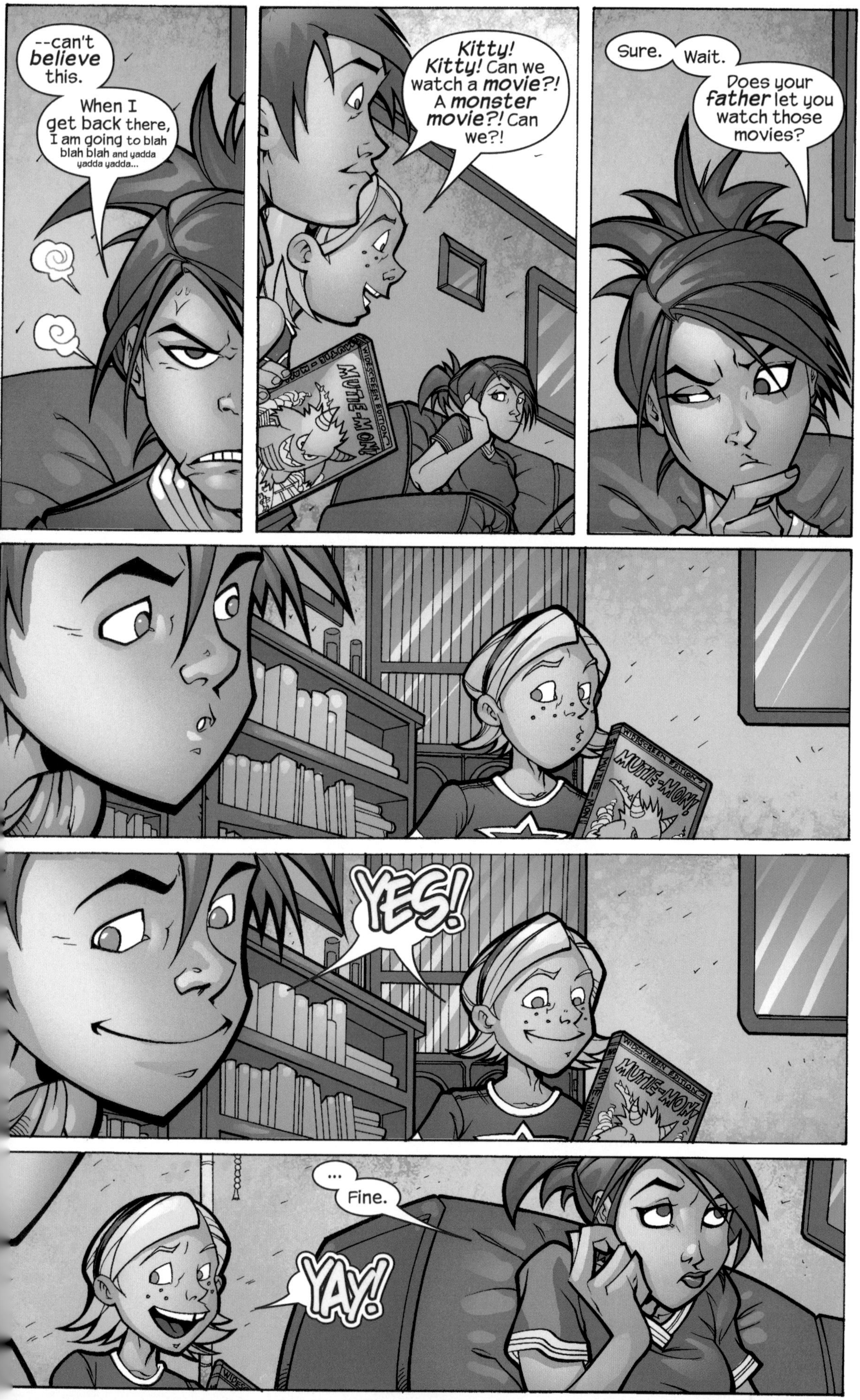
--can't believe this.
When I get back there, I am going to blah blah blah and yadda yadda yadda...
Kitty! Kitty! Can we watch a movie?! A monster movie?! Can we?!
Sure.
Wait.
Does your father let you watch those movies?
YES!
...
Fine.
YAY!

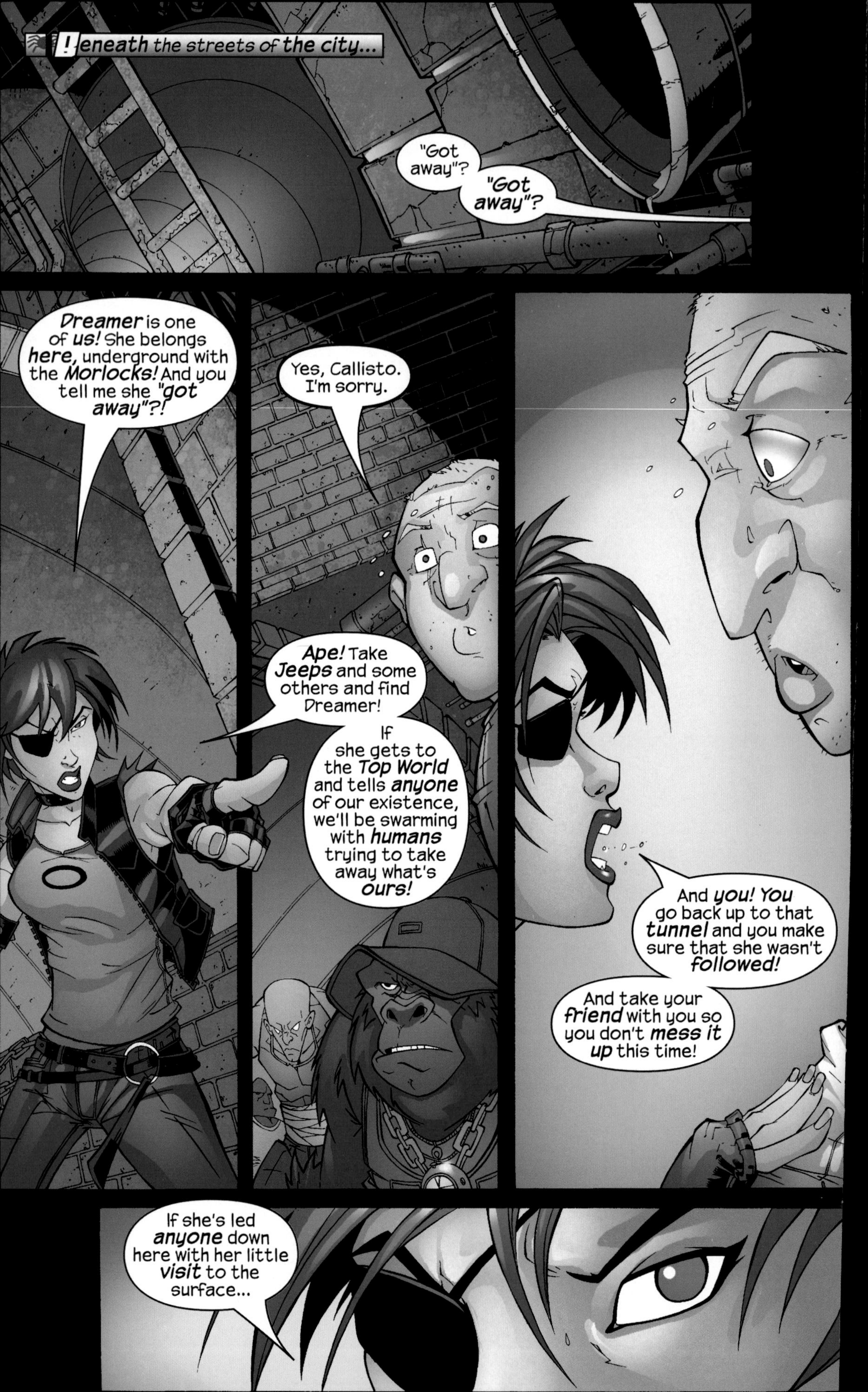

!eneath the streets of the city...
"Got away"?
"Got away"?
Dreamer is one of us! She belongs here, underground with the Morlocks! And you tell me she "got away"?!
Yes, Callisto. I'm sorry.
Ape! Take Jeeps and some others and find Dreamer!
If she gets to the Top World and tells anyone of our existence, we'll be swarming with humans trying to take away what's ours!
And you! You go back up to that tunnel and you make sure that she wasn't followed!
And take your friend with you so you don't mess it up this time!
If she's led anyone down here with her little visit to the surface...

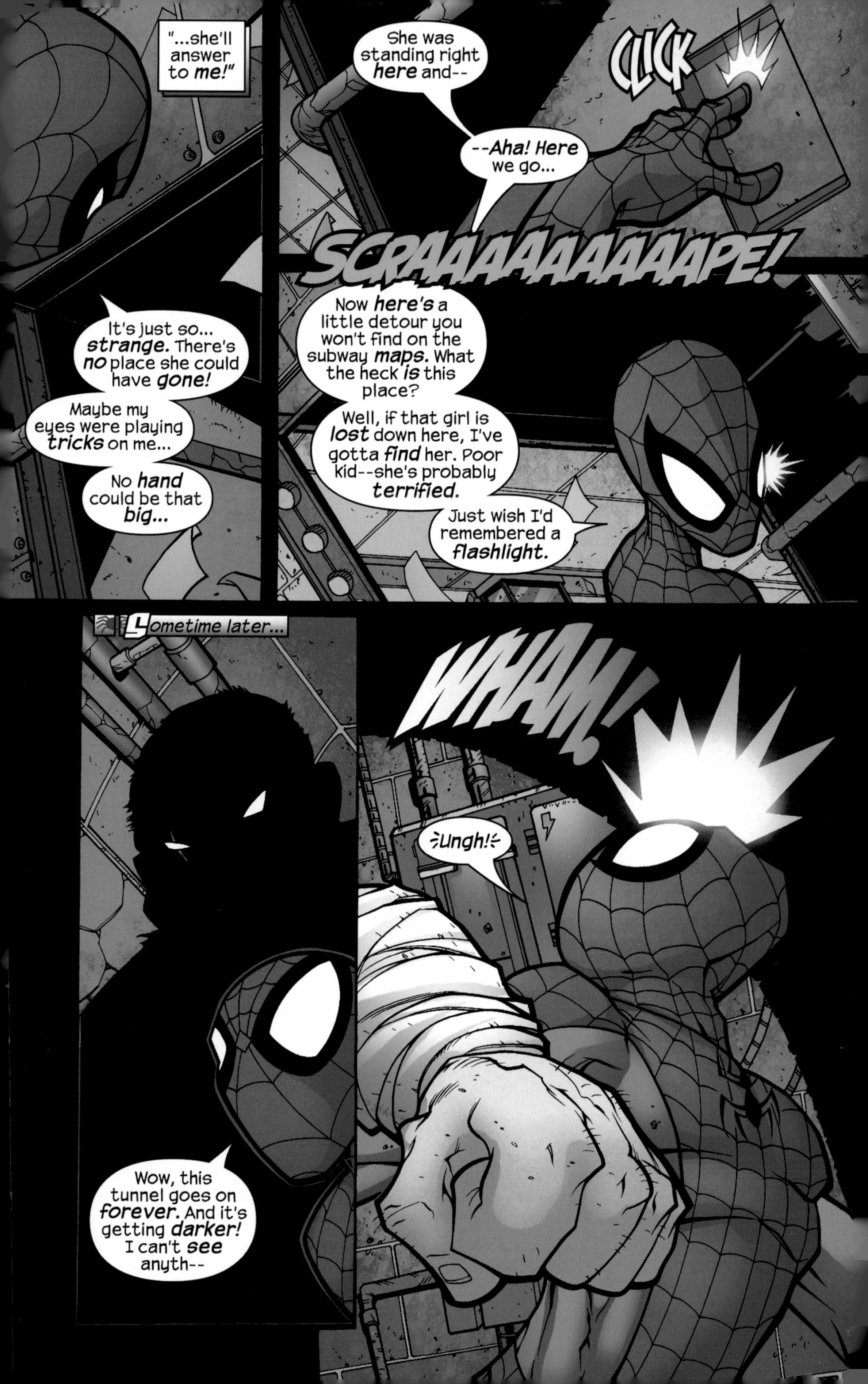
"...she'll answer to me!"
She was standing right here and--
--Aha! Here we go...
CLICK
SCRAAAAAAAAAAPE!
It's just so... strange. There's no place she could have gone!
Maybe my eyes were playing tricks on me...
No hand could be that big...
Now here's a little detour you won't find on the subway maps. What the heck is this place?
Well, if that girl is lost down here, I've gotta find her. Poor kid--she's probably terrified.
Just wish I'd remembered a flashlight.
Sometime later...
Wow, this tunnel goes on forever. And it's getting darker! I can't see anyth--
WHAM!
Ungh!

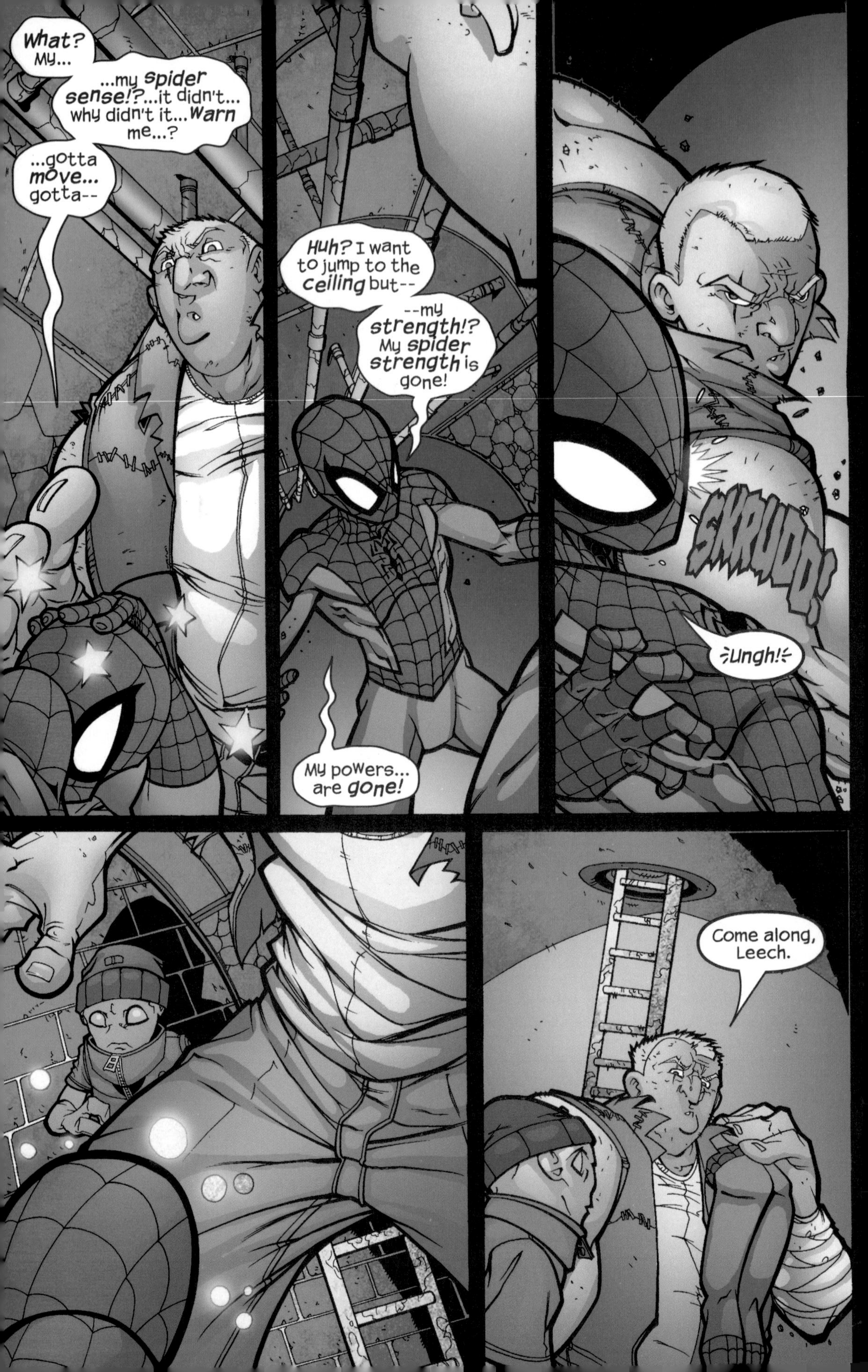
What? My...
...my spider sense!?...it didn't... why didn't it...warn me...?
...gotta move... gotta--
Huh? I want to jump to the ceiling but--
--my strength!? My spider strength is gone!
My powers... are gone!
SKRUDD!
Ungh!
Come along, Leech.

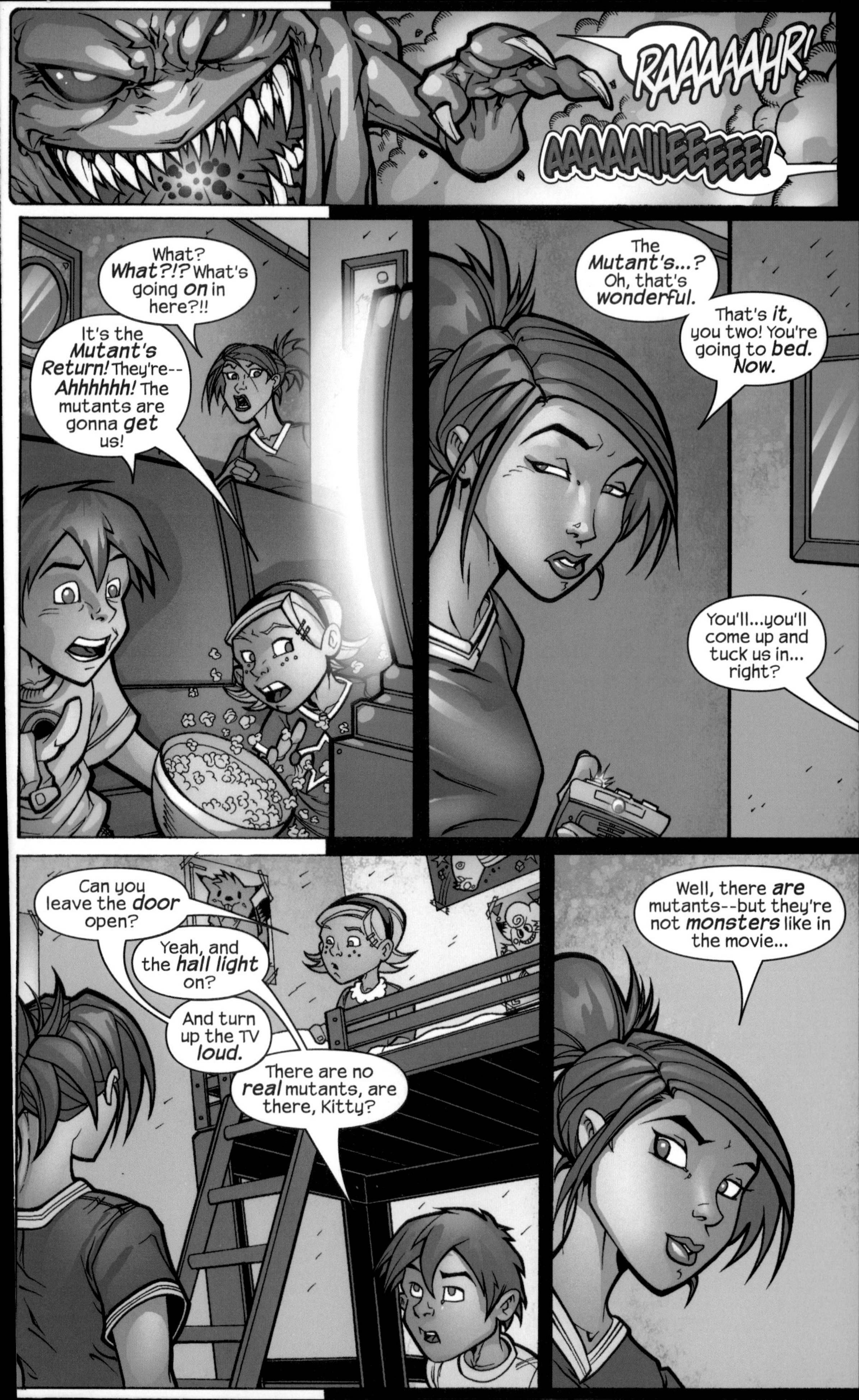
RAAAAAHR!
AAAAAIIIEEEEEE!
What? What?!? What's going on in here?!!
It's the Mutant's Return! They're-- Ahhhhhh! The mutants are gonna get us!
The Mutant's...? Oh, that's wonderful.
That's it, you two! You're going to bed. Now.
You'll...you'll come up and tuck us in... right?
Can you leave the door open?
Yeah, and the hall light on?
And turn up the TV loud.
There are no real mutants, are there, Kitty?
Well, there are mutants--but they're not monsters like in the movie...

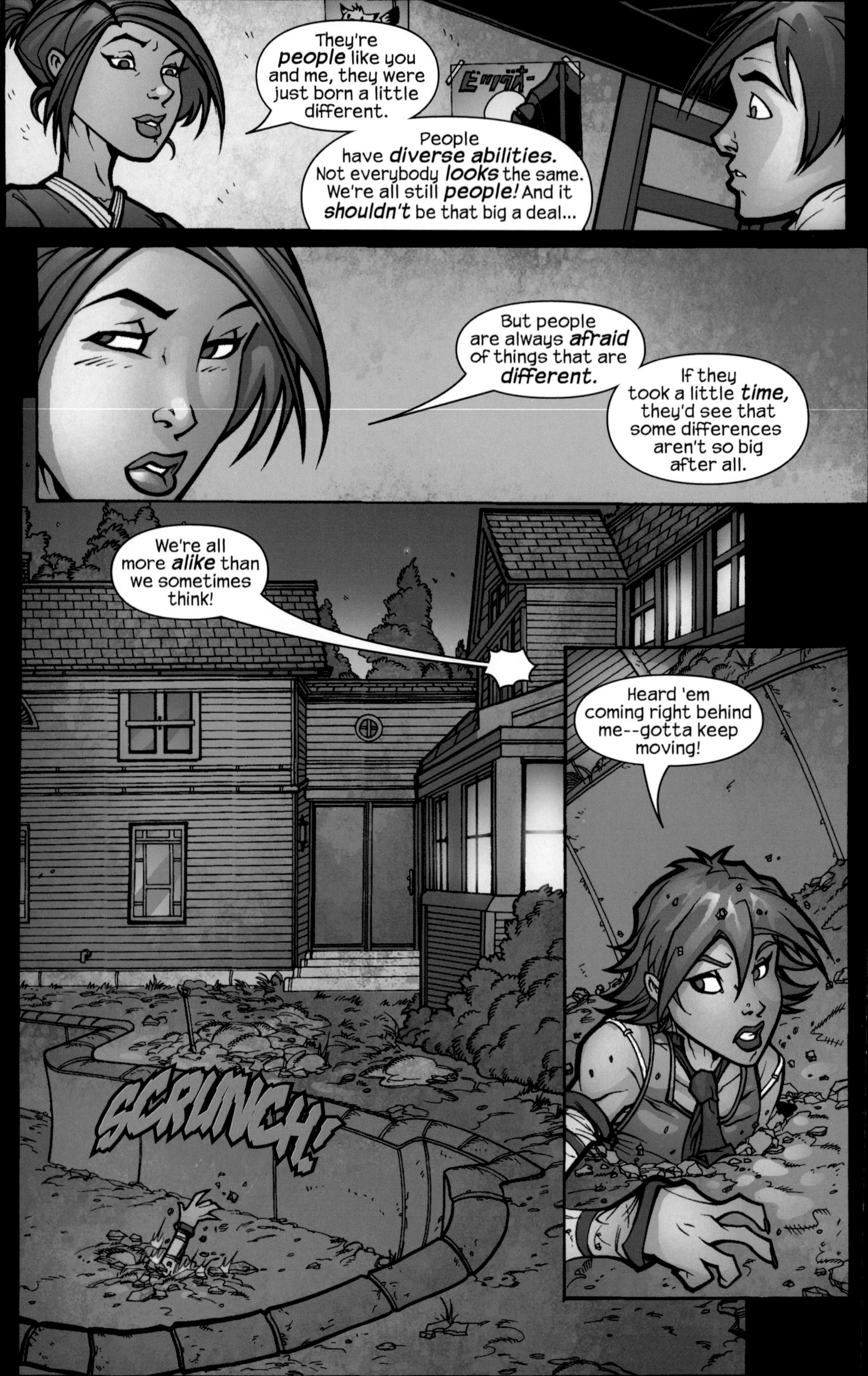
They're *people* like you and me, they were just born a little different.
People have *diverse abilities.* Not everybody *looks* the same. We're all still *people!* And it *shouldn't* be that big a deal...
But people are always *afraid* of things that are *different.*
If they took a little *time,* they'd see that some differences aren't so big after all.
We're all more *alike* than we sometimes think!
SCRUNCH!
Heard 'em coming right behind me--gotta keep moving!

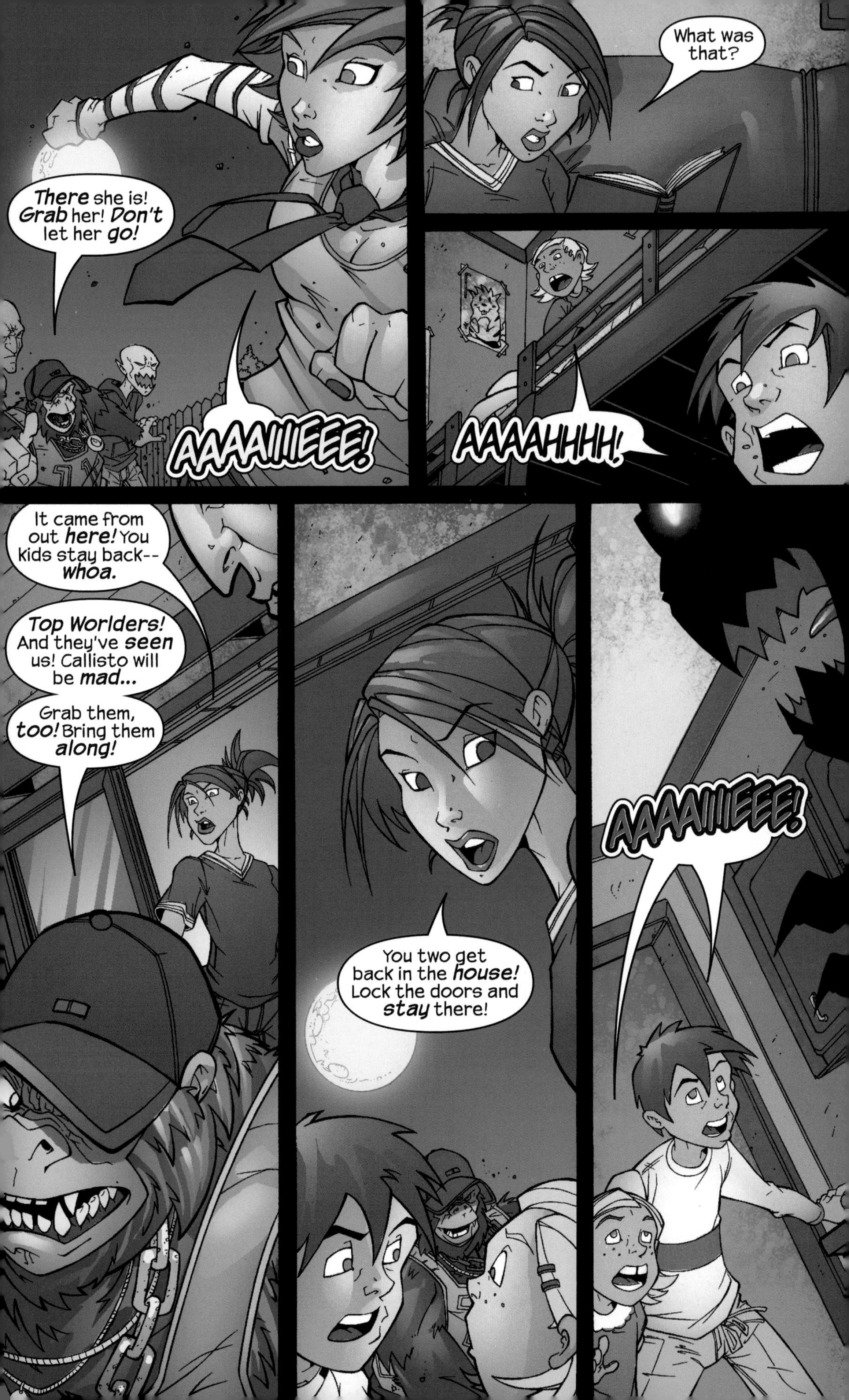

There she is! Grab her! Don't let her go!
AAAAIIIIEEEE!
What was that?
AAAAHHHH!
It came from out here! You kids stay back-- whoa.
Top Worlders! And they've seen us! Callisto will be mad...
Grab them, too! Bring them along!
You two get back in the house! Lock the doors and stay there!
AAAAIIIIEEEE!

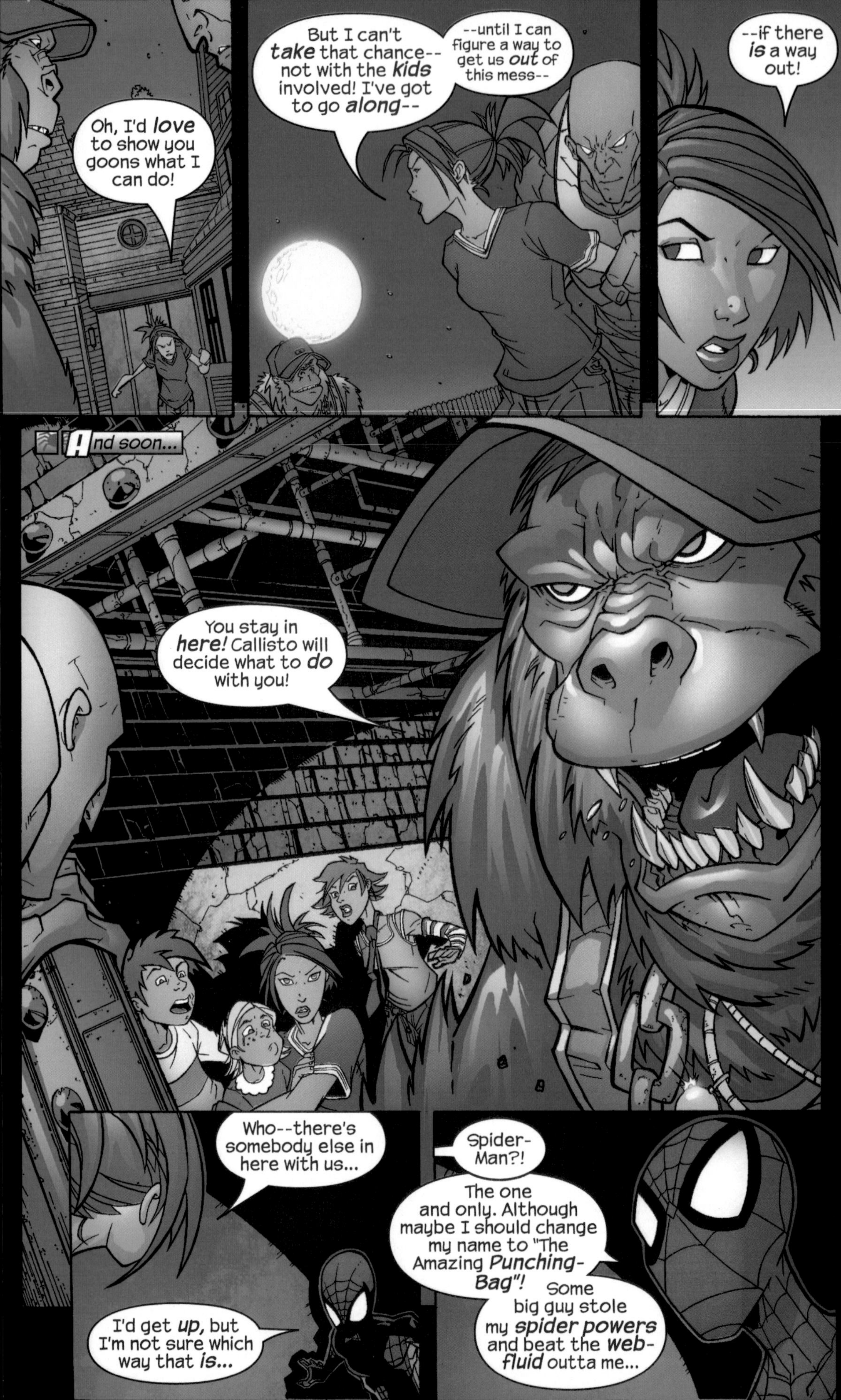

Oh, I'd love to show you goons what I can do!
But I can't take that chance-- not with the kids involved! I've got to go along--
--until I can figure a way to get us out of this mess--
--if there is a way out!
And soon...
You stay in here! Callisto will decide what to do with you!
Who--there's somebody else in here with us...
I'd get up, but I'm not sure which way that is...
Spider-Man?!
The one and only. Although maybe I should change my name to "The Amazing Punching-Bag"!
Some big guy stole my spider powers and beat the web-fluid outta me...

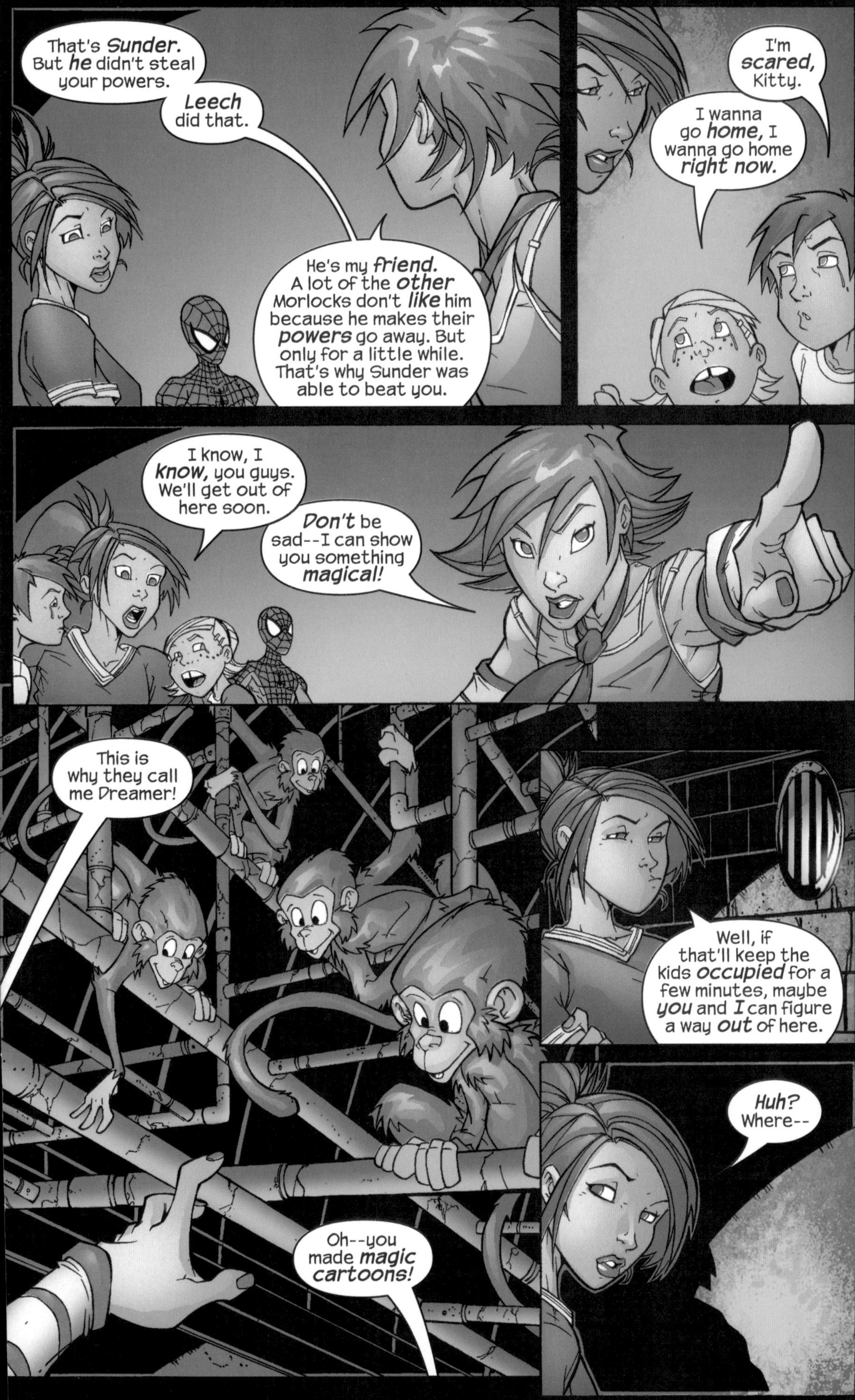
That's Sunder. But he didn't steal your powers.
Leech did that.
He's my friend. A lot of the other Morlocks don't like him because he makes their powers go away. But only for a little while. That's why Sunder was able to beat you.
I'm scared, Kitty.
I wanna go home, I wanna go home right now.
I know, I know, you guys. We'll get out of here soon.
Don't be sad--I can show you something magical!
This is why they call me Dreamer!
Oh--you made magic cartoons!
Well, if that'll keep the kids occupied for a few minutes, maybe you and I can figure a way out of here.
Huh? Where--

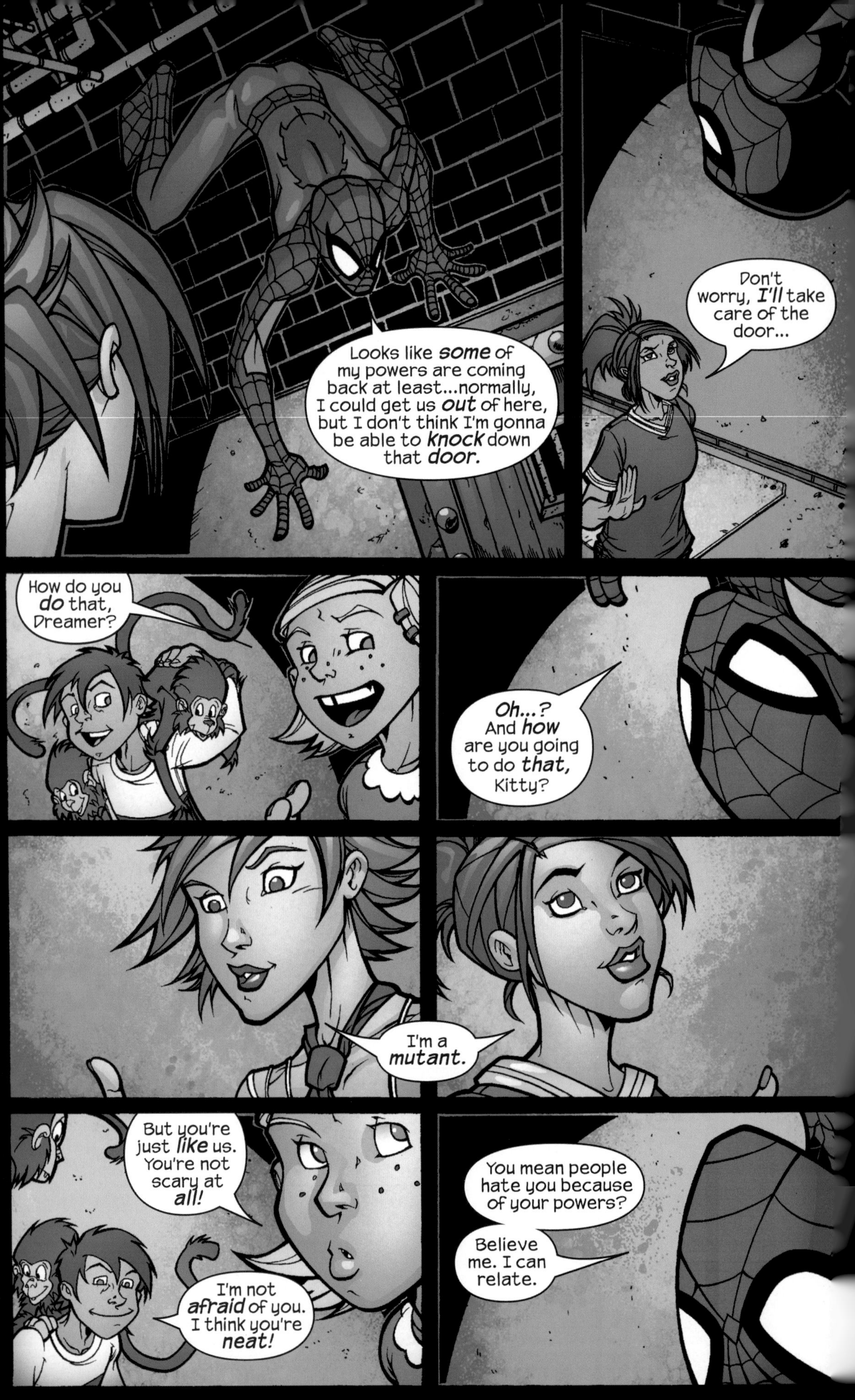
Looks like some of my powers are coming back at least...normally, I could get us out of here, but I don't think I'm gonna be able to knock down that door.
Don't worry, I'll take care of the door...
How do you do that, Dreamer?
Oh...? And how are you going to do that, Kitty?
I'm a mutant.
But you're just like us. You're not scary at all!
I'm not afraid of you. I think you're neat!
You mean people hate you because of your powers?
Believe me. I can relate.

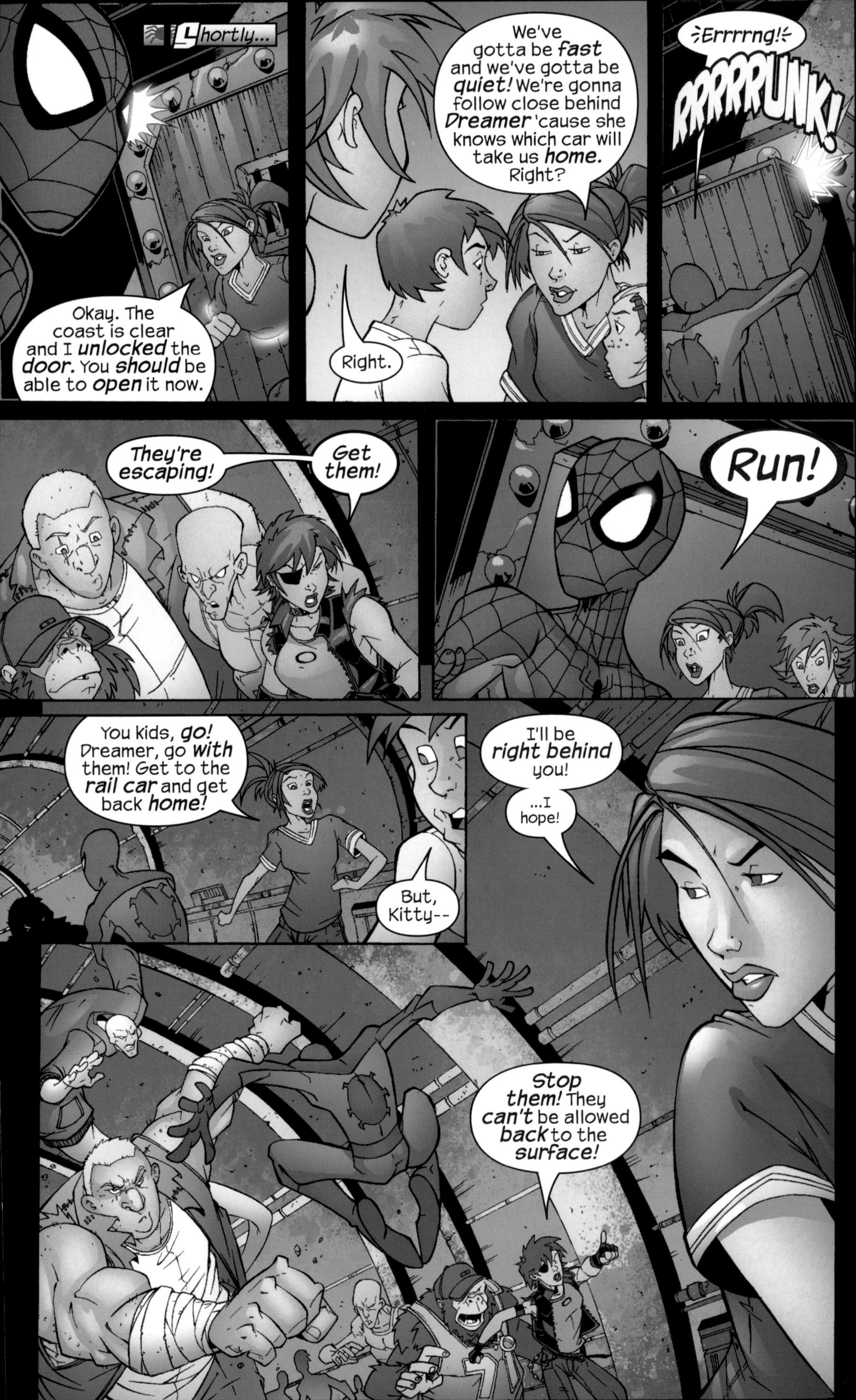

Shortly...
Okay. The coast is clear and I unlocked the door. You should be able to open it now.
We've gotta be fast and we've gotta be quiet! We're gonna follow close behind Dreamer 'cause she knows which car will take us home. Right?
Right.
Errrrng!
RRRRRUNK!
They're escaping!
Get them!
Run!
You kids, go! Dreamer, go with them! Get to the rail car and get back home!
But, Kitty--
I'll be right behind you!
...I hope!
Stop them! They can't be allowed back to the surface!

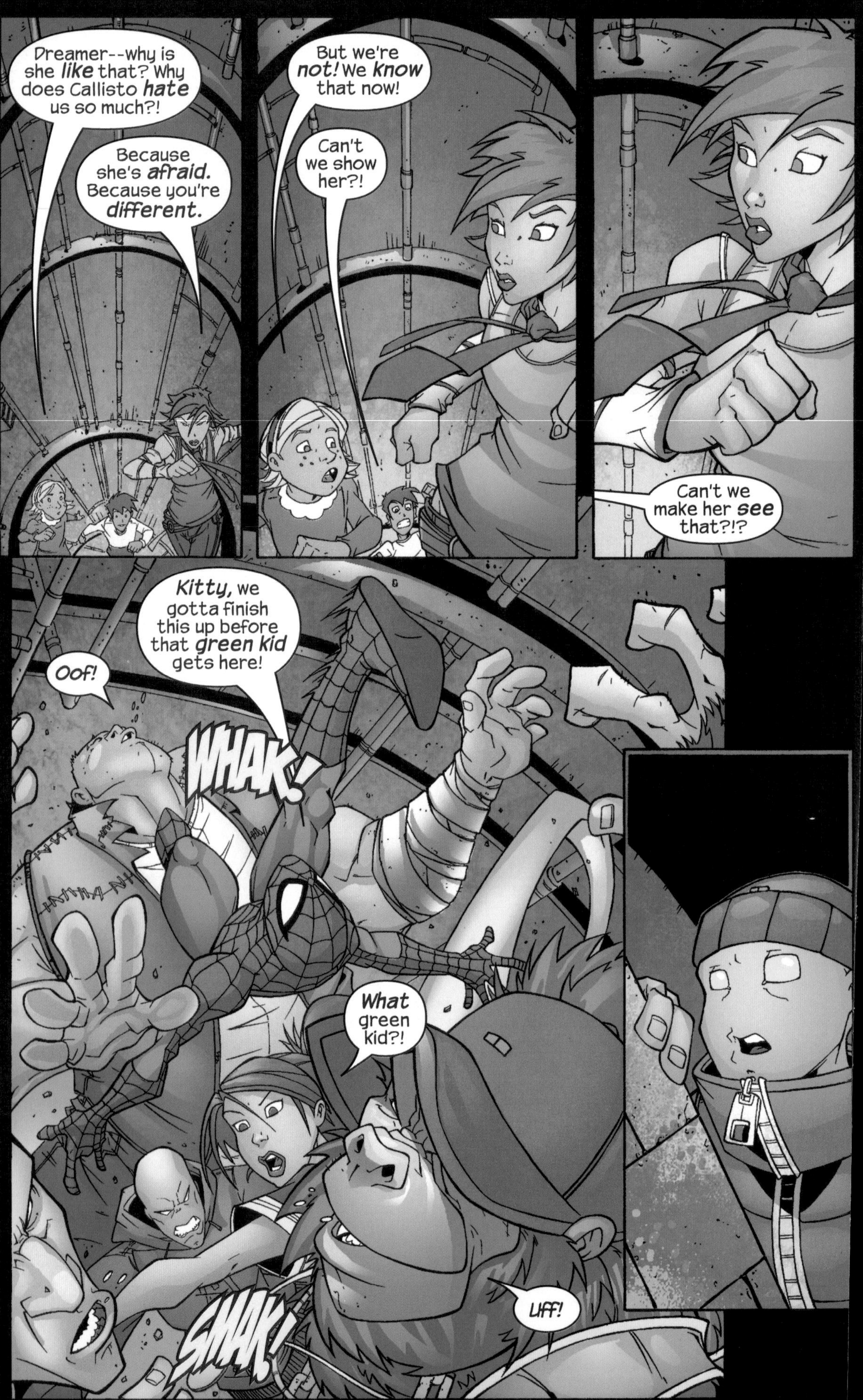
Dreamer--why is she *like* that? Why does Callisto *hate* us so much?!
Because she's *afraid.* Because you're *different.*
But we're *not!* We *know* that now!
Can't we show her?!
Can't we make her *see* that?!?
Kitty, we gotta finish this up before that *green kid* gets here!
Oof!
WHAK!
What green kid?!
UFF!
SMAK!

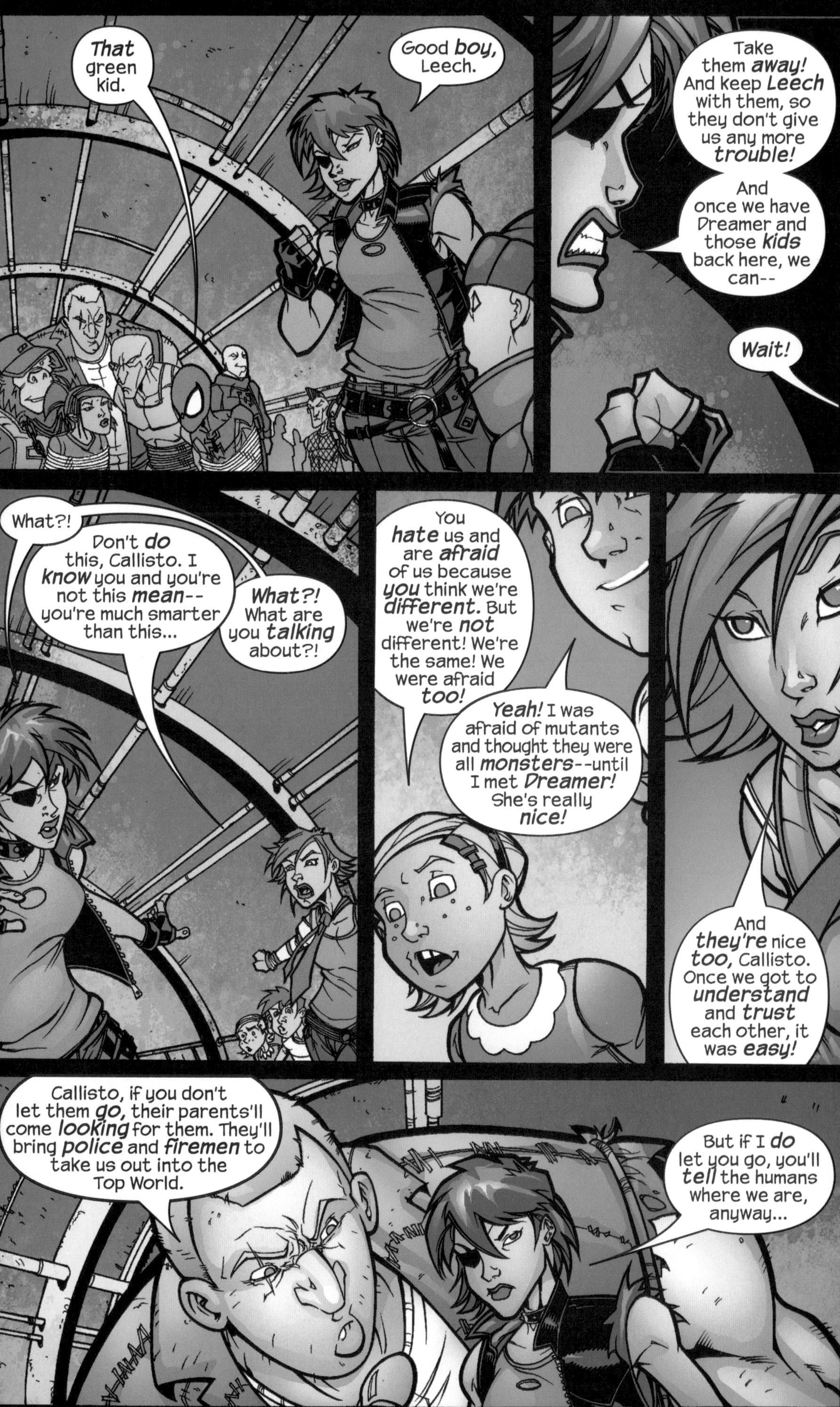

That green kid.
Good boy, Leech.
Take them away! And keep Leech with them, so they don't give us any more trouble!
And once we have Dreamer and those kids back here, we can--
Wait!
What?!
Don't do this, Callisto. I know you and you're not this mean--you're much smarter than this...
What?! What are you talking about?!
You hate us and are afraid of us because you think we're different. But we're not different! We're the same! We were afraid too!
Yeah! I was afraid of mutants and thought they were all monsters--until I met Dreamer! She's really nice!
And they're nice too, Callisto. Once we got to understand and trust each other, it was easy!
Callisto, if you don't let them go, their parents'll come looking for them. They'll bring police and firemen to take us out into the Top World.
But if I do let you go, you'll tell the humans where we are, anyway...

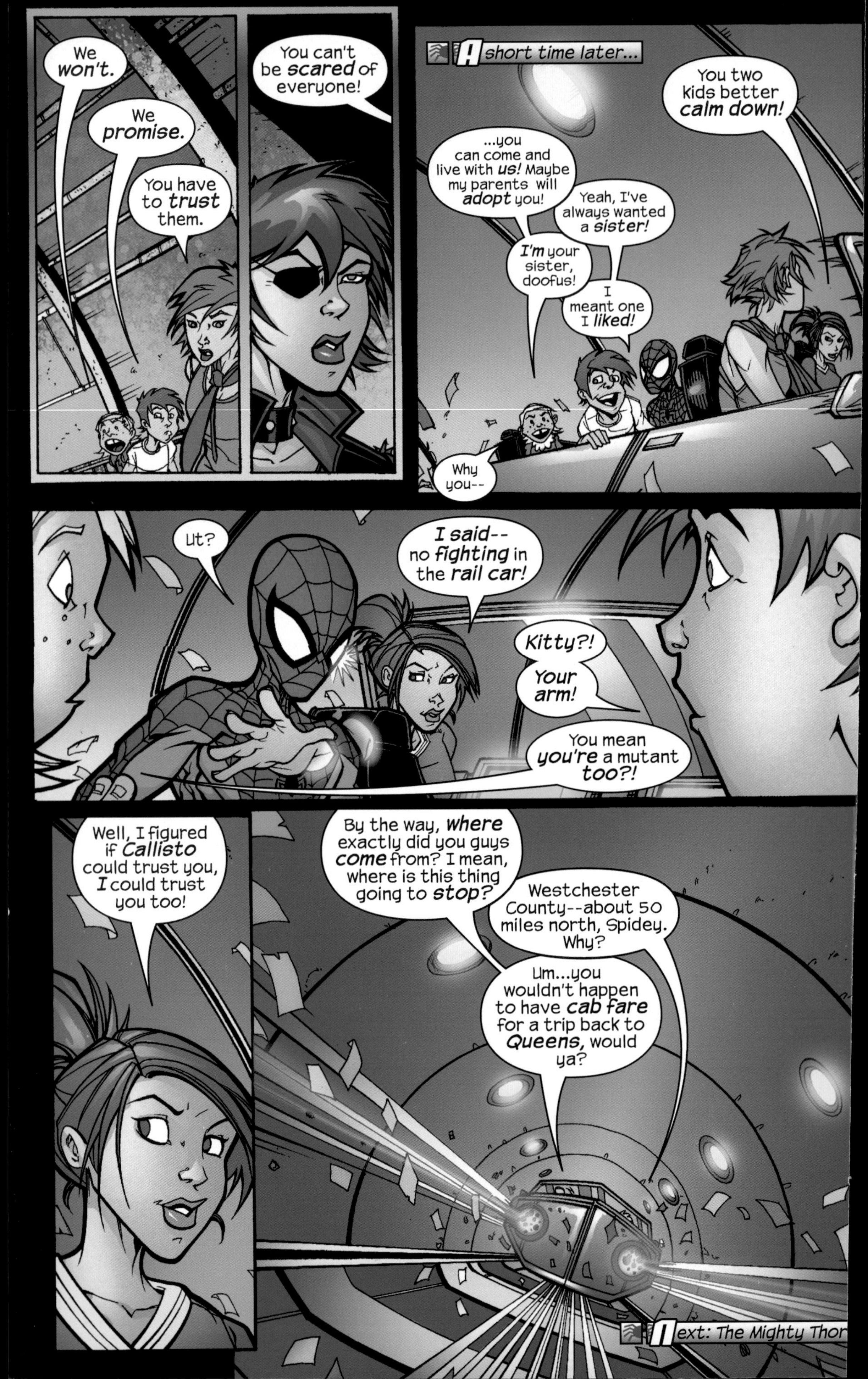
We won't.
We promise.
You have to trust them.
You can't be scared of everyone!
A short time later...
...you can come and live with us! Maybe my parents will adopt you!
Yeah, I've always wanted a sister!
I'm your sister, doofus!
I meant one I liked!
Why you--
You two kids better calm down!
Ut?
I said-- no fighting in the rail car!
Kitty?!
Your arm!
You mean you're a mutant too?!
Well, I figured if Callisto could trust you, I could trust you too!
By the way, where exactly did you guys come from? I mean, where is this thing going to stop?
Westchester County--about 50 miles north, Spidey. Why?
Um...you wouldn't happen to have cab fare for a trip back to Queens, would ya?
Next: The Mighty Thor